HiP & HoP
IN THE HOUSE!

A Free-Flowing
TORTOISE and THE HARE Collection

by jef czekaj

DISNEP • HYPERION
LOS ANGELES   NEW YORK

How to Read This Book!

Whenever you see this rabbit rapping and the words are green, read as **fast fast fast** as you can.

If this turtle is rapping and you see red words, read as s l o o o o o o o o o w l y as you can.

Table of Contents

Hip & Hop, Don't Stop First Hardcover Edition, February 2010
Yes, Yes, Yaul! First Hardcover Edition, May 2012
1 3 5 7 9 10 8 6 4 2
FAC-029191-18173
Printed in Malaysia

This book is set in Janson Pro/Monotype; Garden Gnome/Fontspring.
Designed by Elizabeth H. Clark and Tyler Nevins
Art is created with brush and ink on Bristol board; color is added using Adobe Photoshop
on a Mac

Library of Congress Cataloging-in-Publication Control Number: 2018006750
ISBN 978-1-368-02213-2
Reinforced binding
Visit www.DisneyBooks.com

HiP & HoP
Don't Stop!

by jef czekaj

Disnep • HYPERION

LOS ANGELES   NEW YORK

This is **HOP**. You can probably figure out what kind of animal she is.

BUNNY FOR LIFE!

HOP'S HOUSE

BREAKBEAT MEADOW

SUGAR HILLS

Hip and Hop lived in different parts of Oldskool County. But they had something in common.

They both loved to write rhymes.

My raps are slow.
I take my time.
No need to rush
the words that rhyme.

My shell is hard,
and my skin is green.
I'm the freshest turtle
that you've ever seen.

Hip's raps were slower than molasses.
So slow that he made his friends sleepy.

I swim through the water.
I sleep on the rocks.
When I was three
I caught turtle pox.

I went to the doctor.
He gave me a shot.
Then I felt better,
in fact, quite a lot.

Hop's rhymes were quicker than lightning. So quick that her friends could barely understand her.

I take my bath
in a lake.
My favorite food
is carrot cake.

I jump to the left.
I jump to the right.
When I fall asleep,
I need a night-light.

WHAT DID SHE SAY?

I THINK SOMETHING ABOUT A PARROT SNAKE.

You might think that Hip and Hop were friends.
But they had never even met.
You see, creatures from Slowjamz Swamp
and Breakbeat Meadow didn't talk to each other.

No one could remember exactly why.
It's just the way it was.

One day, on their way home from school, Hip and Hop saw the same poster.

Then, they saw each other.

Hip and Hop didn't know what to do.

Hip was up next.

The swamp is where I make my home. If I had some hair I'd use a comb.

It was getting late,

so they headed their separate ways

The next day, Hop told her classmates about her new friend.

Things didn't go much better with Hip.

They practiced rhyming and listened to their favorite music.

And sometimes, they just did nothing together.

At last, the big day arrived.
It seemed like everyone from Oldskool County was there.

Finally, just two contestants were left.

Hop didn't want to compete against her best friend, but the audience was waiting. So she began.

I'm a rabbit, not a hare.
I'm a bunny, not a bear.
So get out of your chair;
wave those paws in the air.

Her rap was so fast that no one could understand her.

Then it was Hip's turn.

If you're a mouse,
or if you're a whale,
big or small,
just shake your tail.

He rapped so slowly
that everyone stopped
paying attention.

Things were going horribly. Luckily, Hip had an idea.

They would rap together!
First Hop took a verse,

Hip's my pal—
I'll shout it out loud.
I'm not ashamed,
in fact, I'm proud.

then Hip,

Here's a memo
that I need to send:
Hop's a bunny
AND my friend.

and then both at the same time.

In the field
and in the swamp,
listen to our beat.
Our beat goes BOMP!

The crowd was stunned!
They had never heard a turtle and a rabbit rap together.

But Hip and Hop kept going.
And a funny thing happened.

First, one animal
started dancing.

Before long, another
joined in,

and then another,

and another.

Soon the whole crowd was breaking,
popping, and locking to Hip and Hop's rhymes.

When it came time to choose the winner, everyone agreed.
Hip and Hop shared the title of "Best Rappers in Oldskool County."

Hip and Hop were happy to win the contest, but mostly they just wanted to rock the party.

And so they did . . . until way past everyone's bedtimes.

YES, YES, YAUL!

by jef czekaj

DISNEP • HYPERION

LOS ANGELES   NEW YORK

HiP the turtle and HOP the rabbit were best friends and the best rappers in Oldskool County.

It was summertime, so they decided to take their show on the road.

on Turntable Mountain,

and in Lake Boogaloo.

And everywhere they went, animals loved their music.
That is, until the day they played in Sugar Hill Park. . . .

Everybody was having a dope time dancing to the music.

Well, *almost* everybody. One prickly porcupine was not enjoying himself.

After the show, Hip and Hop talked to the mysterious stranger.

DID YOU LIKE OUR SHOW?

NO.

DID YOU LIKE **ANY** OF THE SONGS?

UM, NO.

51

Yaul made his answer very clear.

Hip and Hop decided to throw Yaul the best surprise birthday party Oldskool County had ever seen.

I'll invite baboons,
cool raccoons,
and baby moths
still in cocoons.

Bring your crew,
and I'll bring mine.
And everyone
will dress so fine.

The next afternoon everyone gathered at the park to celebrate.

And, of course, up-and-coming rap acts threw down some songs.

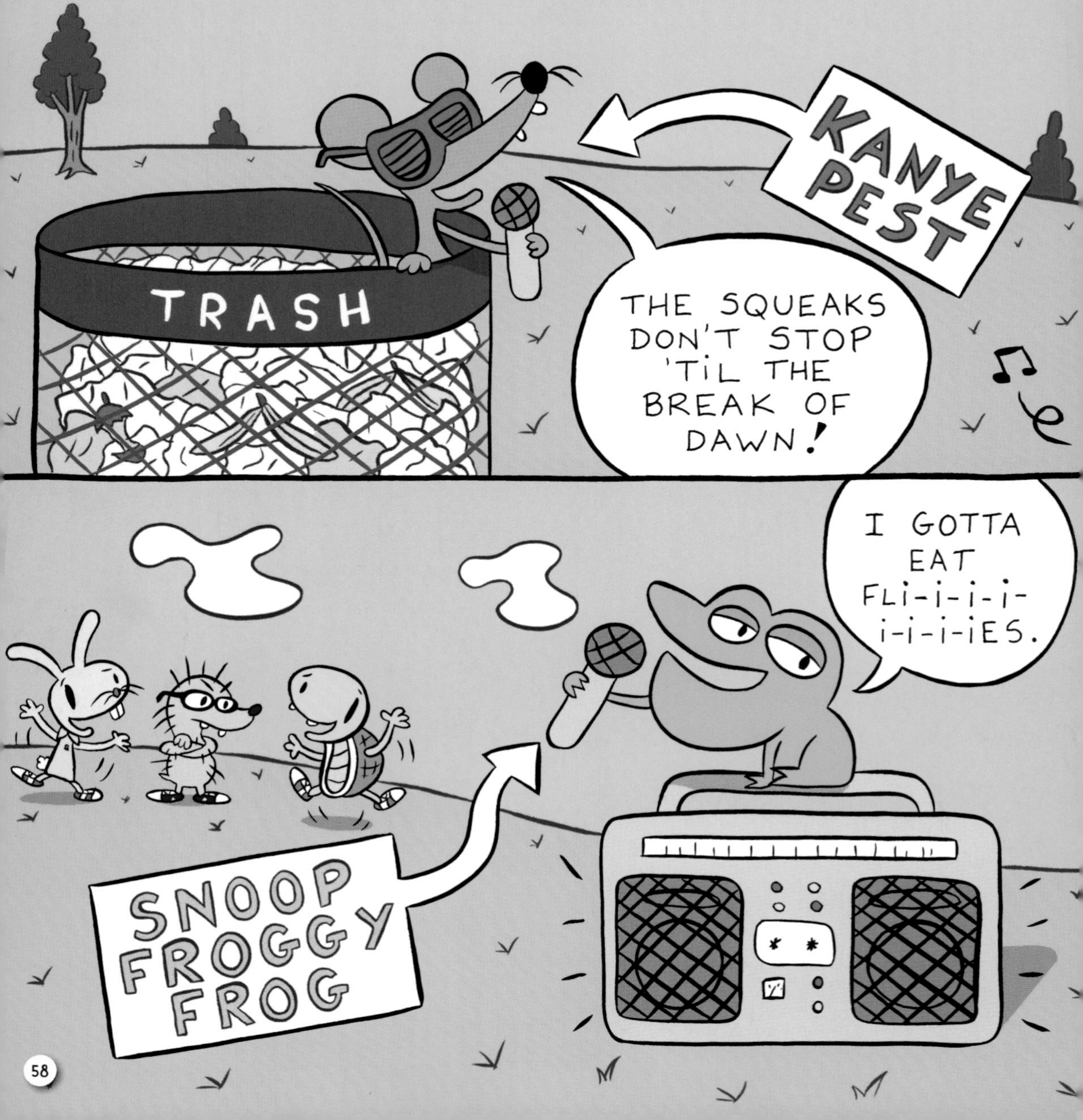

Some animals said it was the best party Oldskool County had ever seen. But the guest of honor was not impressed.

Luckily, his friends and family had one more trick up their sleeves.

Yaul's aunt had made
a special gift for him:
a handmade sweater.

TRY
iT
ON.

WIGGLE

WIGGLE

It was a little small,

POP

and A LOT itchy.

iTCH

iTCH

iTCH

iTCH

He had to get it off as
soon as possible.

SCRATCH

SCRATCH

As Yaul scratched and squirmed in his itchy wool sweater, Hip and Hop rapped.

Go, Yaul, go.
Do your dance.
It looks like ants
are in your pants.

Watch his jumps,
and watch his spins.
All you fresh fish,
throw up your fins!

Finally, he got the sweater off.

BUT I WASN'T DANC–

Yaul realized that moving to the sounds of Hip and Hop's fresh beats actually *had* been fun.

Maybe he didn't *always* have to say no.

And so, for the first time ever, he gave a different answer.

You can probably guess what he said.

The answer was, most definitely, YES!

Bonus mini-comic!

HiP & HoP in:

Record Shopping

by jef czekaj